zrjc
5/11

D1195894

Smithsonian Prehistoric Zone

Woolly Mammoth

by Gerry Bailey
Illustrated by Karen Carr

Crabtree Publishing Company

www.crabtreebooks.com

Crabtree Publishing Company

www.crabtreebooks.com

Author
Gerry Bailey

Illustrator
Karen Carr

Editorial coordinator
Kathy Middleton

Editor
Lynn Peppas

Proofreader
Kathy Middleton

Prepress technician
Samara Parent

Print and production coordinator
Katherine Berti

Copyright © 2010 Palm Publishing LLC and the Smithsonian Institution, Washington DC, 20560 USA
All rights reserved.

Woolly Mammoth, originally published as *Woolly Mammoth in Trouble* by Dawn Bentley, Illustrated by Karen Carr
Book copyright © 2004 Trudy Corporation and the Smithsonian Institution, Washington DC 20560.

Library of Congress Cataloging-in-Publication Data

Bailey, Gerry.
  Woolly mammoth / by Gerry Bailey ; illustrated by Karen Carr.
    p. cm. -- (Smithsonian prehistoric zone)
  Includes index.
  ISBN 978-0-7787-1821-5 (pbk. : alk. paper) -- ISBN 978-0-7787-1808-6
(reinforced library binding : alk. paper) -- ISBN 978-1-4271-9712-2
(electronic (pdf))
  1. Woolly mammoth--Juvenile literature. I. Carr, Karen, 1960- , ill.
II. Title.

QE882.P8B34 2011
569'.67--dc22
                      2010044496

Library and Archives Canada Cataloguing in Publication

Bailey, Gerry
    Woolly mammoth / by Gerry Bailey ; illustrated by Karen Carr.

(Smithsonian prehistoric zone)
Includes index.
At head of title: Smithsonian Institution.
Issued also in electronic format.
ISBN 978-0-7787-1808-6 (bound).--ISBN 978-0-7787-1821-5 (pbk.)

    1. Woolly mammoth--Juvenile literature. I. Carr, Karen, 1960-
II. Smithsonian Institution III. Title. IV. Series: Bailey, Gerry.
Smithsonian prehistoric zone.

QE882.P8B33 2011   j569'.67   C2010-906964-1

Crabtree Publishing Company

www.crabtreebooks.com   1-800-387-7650
Copyright © **2011 CRABTREE PUBLISHING COMPANY.**

Published in the United States
Crabtree Publishing
PMB 59051
350 Fifth Avenue, 59th Floor
New York, New York 10118

Published in Canada
Crabtree Publishing
616 Welland Ave.
St. Catharines, Ontario
L2M 5V6

Printed in China/012011/GW20101014

Dinosaurs

Living things had been around for billions of years before dinosaurs **evolved**. Animal life on Earth started with single-cell **organisms** that lived in the seas. About 380 million years ago, some animals came out of the sea and onto the land. These were the ancestors that would become the mighty dinosaurs.

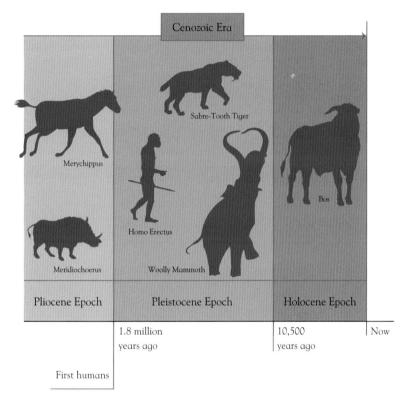

The dinosaur era is called the Mesozoic era. Prehistoric animals lived during the Cenozoic era that came afterward. It is divided into epochs, which are periods of time marked by special characteristics. The Pleistocene epoch lasted from 1.8 million years ago until 10, 500 years ago.

Woolly mammoths lived during the Pleistocene period. Other large mammals, such as woolly rhinoceroses and cave bears, lived then too. Early humans most likely hunted the woolly mammoth. Changes in climate at the end of the last Ice Age led to changes in food supplies. The woolly mammoth became **extinct**.

Woolly Mammoth used his great tusks to dig below
the snow and reach the grass buried underneath.
It was unusual to have this much snow on the ground.

It looked like another storm was coming.
The storm would not bother him, though.
He was used to such cold, Ice Age conditions.

Like the other males in his herd, Woolly Mammoth had a large head. His tusks were long and curved. His trunk was packed with small muscles and was nearly seven feet (two meters) long. At its sensitive tip,

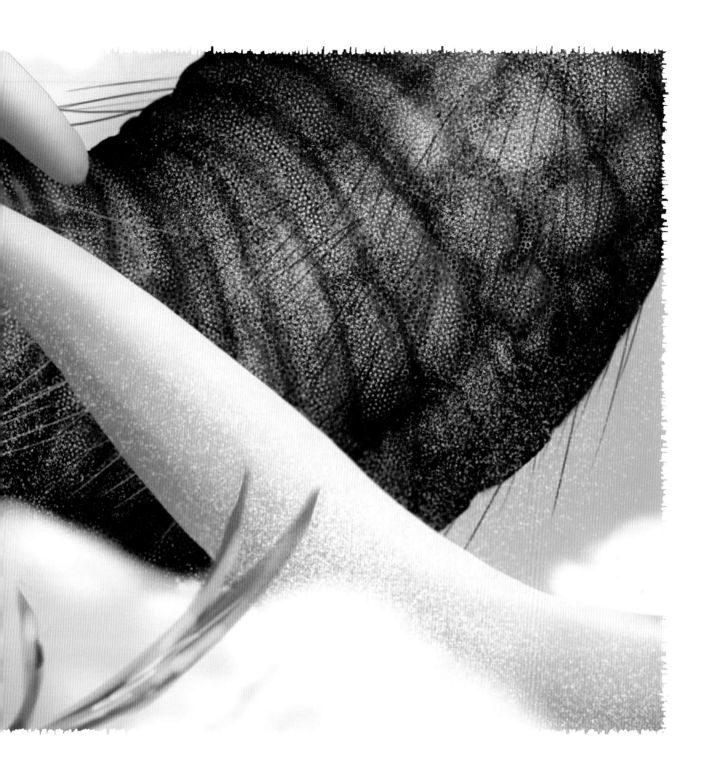

it had two points that acted like human fingers.
They could be used for breaking off short grass,
flowers, or buds. He could wrap his whole trunk
around larger tufts and pull them up.

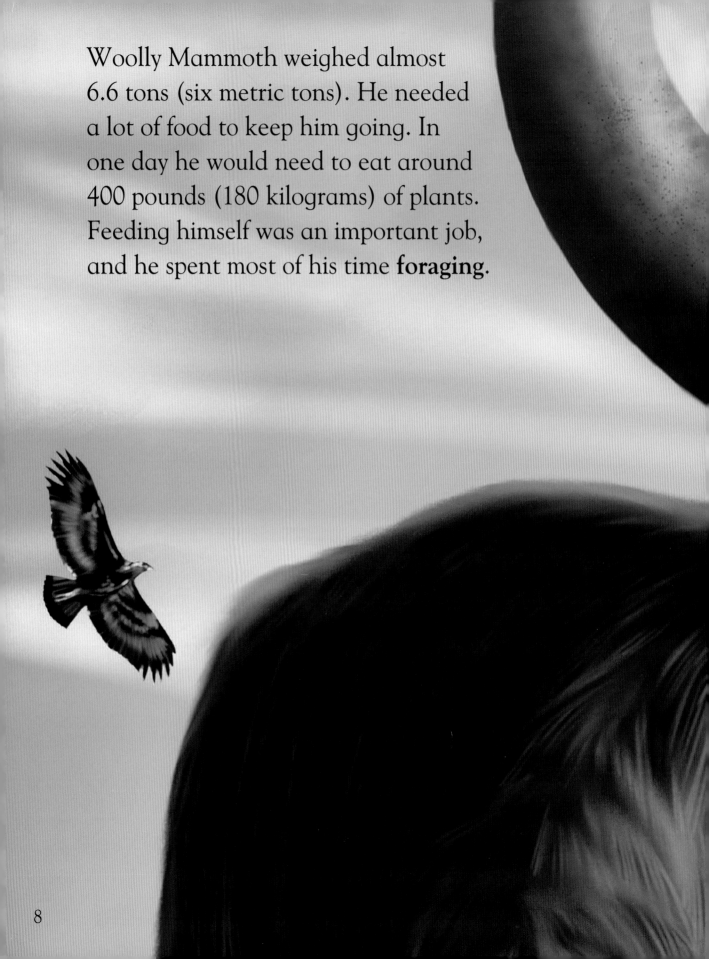

Woolly Mammoth weighed almost 6.6 tons (six metric tons). He needed a lot of food to keep him going. In one day he would need to eat around 400 pounds (180 kilograms) of plants. Feeding himself was an important job, and he spent most of his time **foraging**.

The snowstorm came while Woolly
Mammoth found tasty grass and other
plants to eat. At first he did not notice
the flakes falling.

When he did look up he saw a thick cloud of snow swirling in the air around him. He could just make out two broad-antlered giant deer standing close by, but he could no longer see his herd.

A fox, with its shaggy white winter coat, darted
by as Woolly Mammoth began to plod through
the snow. The huge mammoth knew he must

return to his herd but the storm was getting
worse. He could not see his path. It would be
best if he found a place to sit out the blizzard.

The land around was a rolling, grassy **steppe**.
It was flat, open land with few trees. Sometimes
there were tall cliffs with cave openings that could
provide shelter. Woolly Mammoth was lucky.

He found a cave that was empty. It was
small but it gave him just enough room
to back in. He was sheltered from the
driving snow.

Woolly Mammoth looked out over the snow-covered land when the storm had stopped. He must leave the shelter now and find his herd. He made his way through the snow. He did not see the shadowy form of a sabre-tooth cat prowling along the edge of the cliff. The big cat watched as Woolly Mammoth plodded on.

17

Woolly Mammoth needed to find his herd quickly.
Even though he was big, a lone mammoth was in
danger. His herd offered protection from **predators**.
Woolly Mammoth began to feel uneasy.

He could sense that he was not alone. Then he looked up. Three sabre-tooth cats glared hungrily at him from a nearby ridge. He knew their sabre teeth were sharp enough to **puncture** his thick skin.

Suddenly the cats charged off the ridge and pounced. They attacked Woolly Mammoth from different directions. Woolly Mammoth fought back by swinging his massive tusks from left to right and back again. He used his enormous strength to beat off the ferocious sabre-tooth cats. Then he carried on.

Woolly Mammoth saw a pair of gray wolves behind him. He was not afraid. He saw a line of woolly mammoths making their way through the snow just ahead of him. The wolves would not attack a mammoth with its herd. Woolly Mammoth recognized the scent of his herd. He was home.

Woolly Mammoth raised his long trunk and let out a mighty bellow to get their attention. The herd stopped at once. They recognized the sound as coming from a member of their group. They waited until he took his place in the line. Then, as the snow began to fall again, they marched off.

All about Woolly Mammoth

The woolly mammoth, or *Mammuthus primigenius*, first lived in Siberia, a part of north-eastern Asia, around 250,000 years ago. By 100,000 years ago, it had spread across Europe to the British Isles, and from Asia into North America. It became extinct around 10,000 years ago. A group of smaller, or dwarf, woolly mammoths survived on Wrangel Island in the Arctic Ocean until around 4,000 years ago.

Cave paintings of these elephant-like mammals show that humans and woolly mammoths lived at the same time. The paintings show its long, shaggy fur and curved tusks. The woolly mammoth grew a very long outer layer of dark-colored hair and an inner layer of softer wool. Along with its hair, a thick layer of fat helped to **insulate** it from the cold. Small ears and a short tail helped to **reduce** heat loss.

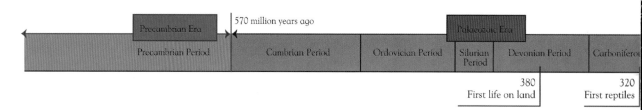

Precambrian Era				Palaeozoic Era		
Precambrian Period	Cambrian Period	Ordovician Period	Silurian Period	Devonian Period		Carboniferou

570 million years ago

380
First life on land

320
First reptiles

A woolly mammoth weighed up to 6.6 tons (six metric tons) and stood nearly 10 feet (three meters) high. It had to eat a lot to support its weight. It ate mostly grass but also steppe vegetation, such as club moss and **sedge**. It also ate other herbs and shrubs. It used its tusks to dig in the snow for plants and its huge **molars** to grind them down.

| Period | Permian Period | Triassic Period | Jurassic Period | Cretaceous Period | | Cenozoic Era | Now |

248

Mesozoic Era

65

Cenozoic Era

Now

1.8
First humans

Mammoth bone huts

During the last Ice Age huge numbers of mammoth bones lay across the ground in eastern Europe. The early humans who lived there at the time made use of these bones because there was very little wood around. They burned the bones to make fires and used them to build huts. Many of these Ice Age shelters have been found in Russia, Ukraine, and Poland.

Mammoth bone huts were between 13 feet (4 meters) and 23 feet (7 meters) across. Sometimes they were built in rows. Other times they were arranged in circles. They were constructed from mammoth bones and covered with hide. Skulls, shoulder blades, and other large bones were used to make a base, or foundation. Tusks were set up to make a porch-like entrance. The roof was probably made of wooden frames covered in animal skins or **turf**.

At a place called Mezherich in the Ukraine a hut was found that used 385 mammoth bones. Some of these bones were up to 6.5 feet (two meters) long. The builders had used skulls, **pelvis**, and leg bones to form the base of the wall. Leg bones and tusks formed the upper wall. Tusks may also have been used to hold down the roof hides. The hut was nearly 16 feet (five meters) in **diameter** and was built 15,000 years ago.

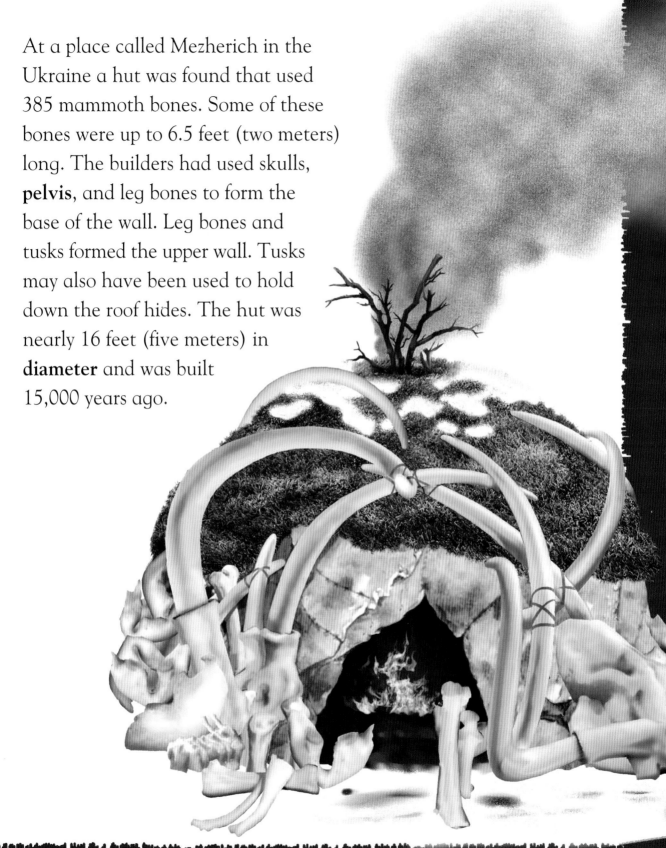

Ice Age animals

The Pleistocene epoch began around 1.8 million years ago and lasted until 10,500 years ago. Sometimes this period is called the period of the Ice Age. There were many different stretches of cold climate within it. Warm periods when the climate was similar to ours were called interglacials. These came in between the cold periods. The last Ice Age period began 100,000 years ago and lasted until around 10,000 years ago. During this time huge sheets of ice slowly pushed south and covered much of the land in North America and Europe. Animals that lived in the northern regions of the world, such as the mammoth, had to adapt to the cold. Over generations it developed a long outer coat of dark hair and an undercoat of fine hair, or wool.

Another animal with a long shaggy coat was the woolly rhinoceros, or *Coelodonta*. It was about 13 feet (4 meters) long with humped shoulders and a coat of shaggy hair to keep it warm in the harsh conditions. Early humans must have hunted this animal, as it is shown on the walls of caves in southern France—in pictures painted around 30,000 years ago.

The cave bear often dealt with the cold by **hibernating** in caves during the worst of the weather. It seems that many bears slept together in the caves, as large amounts of fossil bones have been found together.

A giant deer called *Megaloceros* lived alongside the woolly mammoth and woolly rhinoceros. It is sometimes called the Irish elk. It lived in areas from the United Kingdom to China and Siberia. It had huge flat antlers that measured up to 12 feet (3.7 meters) across.

Glossary

diameter The width of something that is round

evolve To slowly grow and change

extinct No longer living on Earth

forage To search for food

hibernate A lengthy period of sleep that some animals experience during cold weather

insulate To surround something with a special material that stops heat from escaping

molar A tooth that is used to grind food

organism Any living animal or plant

pelvis A basin-shaped bone that joins to the legs

predator An animal that hunts other animals

puncture To make a hole, or break through, with a pointed object

reduce To make less or bring down

sedge Grasslike plants

steppe A grass-covered flat area of land

turf The top layer of soil where grasses and small plants grow

Index

Further Reading and Websites

Woolly Mammoth, Illustrated by Mick Manning, and Brita Granstrom, 2009

Uncovering the Mysterious Woolly Mammoth by Michael Oard, 2007

Websites:

www.smithsonianeducation.org